My Dream of Martin Luther King

My Dream of Martin Luther King

by Faith Ringgold

Crown Publishers, Inc., New York

This book is lovingly dedicated to my brother Andrew Louis Jones, Jr.
and to all the young men and women whose dreams were nightmares.
I pray you are now resting in peace.

Acknowledgments

Many thanks to my daughter Barbara Wallace and her three little girls, Faith, Theodora, and Martha,
who loaned me books from their library about Martin Luther King; Nashameh Lindo, who loaned me her
video from her collection on King; my daughter Michele Wallace,
who enlightened me about Martin Luther King's childhood;
my editor, Simon Boughton, who first suggested that my next book for Crown be about Martin Luther
King; and my mother, Willi Posey, who taught me to dream with my eyes wide open.

Published by Crown Publishers, Inc., a Random House company,
201 East 50th Street, New York, New York 10022
CROWN is a trademark of Crown Publishers, Inc.

Manufactured in the United States of America

Library of Congress Cataloging-in-Publication Data
Ringgold, Faith.
My dream of Martin Luther King / Faith Ringgold. — 1st ed.
p.   cm.
Summary: The author recounts the life of Martin Luther King
in the form of her own dream.
1. King, Martin Luther, Jr., 1929-1968—Juvenile literature. 2. Afro-Americans—
Biography—Juvenile literature. 3. Civil rights workers—United States—Biography—
Juvenile literature. 4. Baptists—United States—Clergy—Biography—Juvenile
literature. [1. King, Martin Luther, Jr., 1929-1968. 2. Civil rights workers. 3. Clergy.
4. Afro-Americans—Biography.] I. Title.
E185.97.K5R56   1995
323'.092—dc20[B]   95-4685
ISBN 0-517-59976-7 (trade)
0-517-59977-5 (lib. bdg.)
10 9 8 7 6 5 4 3 2 1
First Edition

I've always been a dreamer. But the only dreams I can remember are the ones I dream with my eyes wide open. Once I go to sleep, I rarely remember my dreams. However, one day while watching a television program about Martin Luther King, Jr., I slept and had a dream that I will never forget.

In my dream, Martin appeared first as a child in a place so huge that it encompassed the whole world and all its people. There were children and old folks, men and women of all colors, races, and religions. They carried bags containing their prejudice, hate, ignorance, violence, and fear, which they intended to trade for hope, freedom, peace, awareness, and love. Some people had bigger bags than others, but everybody had something to trade.

In this place there were steps that led right up to a light shining bright in the sky. Young Martin and his father, Daddy King, his mother, his grandmother, Mother Dear, and his brother and sister, A.D. and Christine, led the climb up the steps to reach the light. Everyone was singing the words of the old hymn, "We shall overcome. We shall overcome someday."

Then a terrible thing happened. Young Martin's family disappeared, and he was left alone except for his closest friend, a boy who lived across the street, and the boy's mother. They were standing on the school steps when the boy's mother told Young Martin to go away.

"This is a school for white children," she said.

"But I am starting school now too," Young Martin replied proudly.

"You must go to the colored school," she barked.

"But why?" asked Young Martin.

"Because we are white and you are black," the boy's mother answered.

Then Young Martin saw a policeman. The policeman was the same one who once called Daddy King a boy. "This is a boy," Daddy King said, pointing to Young Martin. "And I am a man. My name is Reverend King." The policeman said no more, and Daddy King drove away.

But in my dream, Young Martin was alone, and the policeman ran after him, swinging a club and yelling, "Halt, boy! Halt, boy!"

Young Martin ran as fast as he could. He saw a bus and got on it. The bus driver was the same one who had made Martin and his teacher stand up so that white people could sit down. In my dream, the bus driver roared at Young Martin, "There are no seats on this bus for Negroes!"

Young Martin ran from the bus into a crowd of people who were
marching and carrying signs protesting segregated buses.

Young Martin was happy to read the signs calling for freedom and justice.

Because these were problems facing his people, Young Martin joined the
demonstrators, who were singing, "Ain't gonna let nobody turn me around."

But then police on horseback trampled the peaceful demonstrators, and police on foot turned water hoses on them, knocking them down. They attacked them with dogs and beat them with cattle prods. Drenched, ragged, and bleeding, the crowd stopped marching and singing.

Young Martin and all the demonstrators were arrested and thrown into police wagons and taken to jail. While in jail, Young Martin remembered what his mother had told him about slavery and lynching—and that, despite the bad treatment his people received, he was as good as anyone.

Mother Dear came to get Young Martin. She took him in her arms, and he told her about all the awful things that had happened to him and asked her why.

"Although you are only six years old, you can't accept the way things are. You want to find a way to change things, and you will," said Mother Dear.

"But not now. Today is Sunday, and we are going to Sunday school and church. Daddy King will preach a sermon and your mother will direct the choir and you will sing 'Amazing Grace.'"

In my dream, as Young Martin sat in church that day listening to Daddy King preach, there appeared in front of him a very small but powerful holy man from India named Mahatma Gandhi. Gandhi told Young Martin about the power of love to create change and about how he had led more than 300 million of his people to freedom through peaceful resistance.

Young Martin had found the answer to helping his people in Gandhi's teachings.

Now Martin no longer appeared in my dream as a child but as a minister of his own church with a beautiful wife and four children. Many people came to ask the great man to help them. The first was a woman who had been arrested for not giving up her seat on a bus to a white man. Her name was Rosa Parks.

A large meeting was called to protest Rosa Parks's arrest. The group called for a boycott of segregated buses, sit-ins at segregated lunch counters, voter registration so that all black people could vote, equal education for all the children, decent housing, and jobs for all the people.

The group's name was the Southern Christian Leadership Conference and King was its leader. He led his people to the nation's capital, where he spoke with such a powerfully resonant voice that everyone was deeply moved.

"I have a dream that one day this nation will rise up and live out the true meaning of its creed...."

King painted a picture of his dream, saying "I have a dream that one day on the red hills of Georgia the sons of former slaves and the sons of former slave owners will be able to sit down together at the table of brotherhood....

"I have a dream today!"

In my dream I could see King's four little children looking up at King's vision of a better world.

And then King appeared in my dream with black people and white people sitting together on buses and eating at lunch counters and voting together and with the children going to school together and living together, and King was very happy.

But suddenly there was a noise like a firecracker, and I knew
Martin Luther King was dead. In my dream, people were crying,
just as we had on the day he was killed.

Daddy King, Mother, Mother Dear, A.D., Christine, King's wife,
Coretta, his four children, and his many friends and supporters came
to light an eternal flame in memory of the slain hero.

Even the President of the United States was there. The entire world was
in mourning.

And, as dreams go, suddenly I was back in that huge place with men, women, and children of all colors, races, and religions. This time we had come to mourn Martin Luther King's death by trading in bags containing our prejudice, hate, ignorance, violence, and fear for the slain hero's dream.

We emptied the bags onto a great pile, and as the last bag was dumped, the pile exploded into a fire so bright that it lit up the whole world. There, emblazoned across the sky, were the words: EVERY GOOD THING STARTS WITH A DREAM.

A hushed silence came over us as we heard Martin Luther King's words resound through the air. The sound of his voice was so clear in my dream that it woke me up. When I opened my eyes, King was there on the TV screen, and he was saying, "...And He's allowed me to go up to the mountain. And I've looked over. And I've seen the promised land. I may not get there with you. But I want you to know tonight, that we, as a people, will get to the promised land."

The Life of Dr. Martin Luther King, Jr.

January 15, 1929 Martin Luther King, Jr., is born in Atlanta, Georgia.

September 1935 Martin Luther King begins school at the all-black Yonge Street Elementary School in Atlanta.

June 1944 Martin Luther King enters Morehouse College in Atlanta.

February 1948 Martin Luther King is ordained as a Baptist minister. After graduating from Morehouse College in June, he enters the Crozer Theological Seminary in Chester, Pennsylvania.

June 18, 1953 Martin Luther King and Coretta Scott are married.

October 1954 Martin Luther King becomes pastor of the Dexter Avenue Church in Montgomery, Alabama.

June 1955 Martin Luther King receives his Ph.D. in theology from Boston University.

November 17, 1955 Yolanda Denise King, the Kings' first child, is born.

December 1, 1955 Mrs. Rosa Parks refuses to give up her bus seat to a white man in Montgomery, Alabama.

December 5, 1955 Martin Luther King is elected president of the Montgomery Improvement Association and leads a yearlong boycott of the Montgomery buses.

January 26, 1956 Martin Luther King is arrested for the first time, for a traffic violation.

January 1957 Founding of the Southern Christian Leadership Conference (SCLC). Martin Luther King is chosen president.

October 23, 1957 Martin Luther King III is born.

February 1959 Martin Luther King and Coretta Scott King visit India, where they study Mahatma Gandhi's methods of nonviolent protest.

January 1960 The King family moves to Atlanta, where Martin Luther King becomes co-pastor of the Ebenezer Baptist Church with his father, Martin Luther King, Sr.

February 1960 Students in Greensboro, North Carolina, stage the first "sit-ins" at "whites-only" lunch counters.

October 19, 1960 Martin Luther King is jailed after being arrested at a sit-in at a lunch counter in Atlanta.

January 30, 1961 Dexter Scott King is born.

May 1961 "Freedom riders" leave Washington, D.C., by Greyhound bus. The bus is burned by opponents of desegregation, and the riders are beaten upon arrival in Birmingham, Alabama.

December 1961 Martin Luther King joins protestors seeking to desegregate stores and other public places in Albany, Georgia.

September 1962 Black student James Meredith attempts to enroll at the all-white University of Mississippi.

March 28, 1963 Bernice Albertine King is born.

April 12, 1963 Martin Luther King is arrested and jailed (for the thirteenth time) during a march in Birmingham, Alabama.

May 1963 Dogs and fire hoses are used by police in Birmingham to stop protests.

August 28, 1963 250,000 people demonstrate in Washington, D.C., in support of civil rights. Martin Luther King meets with President John F. Kennedy and delivers his "I Have a Dream" speech.

November 22, 1963 President Kennedy is assassinated.

August 1964 Three young civil rights workers are found murdered in Philadelphia, Mississippi.

December 1964 Martin Luther King receives the Nobel Peace Prize.

March 1965 Martin Luther King and the SCLC begin a voter registration campaign in Alabama. Civil rights protestors attempting to march from Selma, Alabama, to Montgomery, Alabama, are beaten by state patrolmen.

August 1965 The 1965 Voting Rights Act is signed by President Lyndon B. Johnson.

March 28, 1968 Martin Luther King leads a march in support of striking sanitation workers in Memphis, Tennessee.

April 3, 1968 Martin Luther King delivers his last speech, "I've Been to the Mountaintop."

April 4, 1968 Martin Luther King is shot and killed at the Lorraine Motel in Memphis. Escaped convict James Earl Ray is later found guilty of the murder.

Bibliography

Bearing the Cross: Martin Luther King and the Southern Christian Leadership Conference by David J. Garrow (New York: Random House, 1986)

Let the Trumpet Sound: The Life of Martin Luther King, Jr. by Stephen B. Oates (New York: Harper & Row, 1982)

Martin Luther King, Jr.: A Documentary...Montgomery to Memphis edited by Flip Schulke (New York: W. W. Norton, 1976)

Martin Luther King, Jr.: To the Mountaintop by William Roger Witherspoon (New York: Doubleday, 1985)

My Life with Martin Luther King, Jr. by Coretta Scott King (New York: Henry Holt, 1993)

About the Author

Faith Ringgold was born in Harlem in 1930, the youngest of three children. She graduated from high school in 1948 and attended the City College of New York. Because women were not allowed to attend City College's School of Liberal Arts at that time, she graduated from the School of Education and went on to become a teacher of art.

Faith Ringgold began painting professionally during the 1960s. During the 1970s, she began incorporating beads and fabric into her work, and in 1980 she created her first painted quilt, "Echoes of Harlem." The project was a collaboration with her mother, Willi Posey, a dressmaker and fashion designer. In "Who's Afraid of Aunt Jemima?" (1983), she incorporated a written story into one of her quilts for the first time. Since then, she has made more than 75 painted "story quilts."

Tar Beach, Faith Ringgold's first book for children, based on a story quilt of the same name, won the Coretta Scott King Award for Illustration and was named a 1992 Caldecott Honor Book. She has written and illustrated two other books for children, *Aunt Harriet's Underground Railroad in the Sky* and *Dinner at Aunt Connie's House*. Her autobiography, *We Flew Over the Bridge: The Memoirs of Faith Ringgold*, was published in 1995.

Today, Ms. Ringgold divides her time between Englewood, New Jersey, and La Jolla, California, where she is a professor of fine art at the University of California at San Diego. She is married to Burdette Ringgold and has two daughters, Barbara and Michele Wallace, and three granddaughters, Faith, Teddy, and Martha.